Can you find these?
10 beetles
11 butterflies
2 cicadas
1 caterpillar
4 nests

BOWERBIRD BROOD

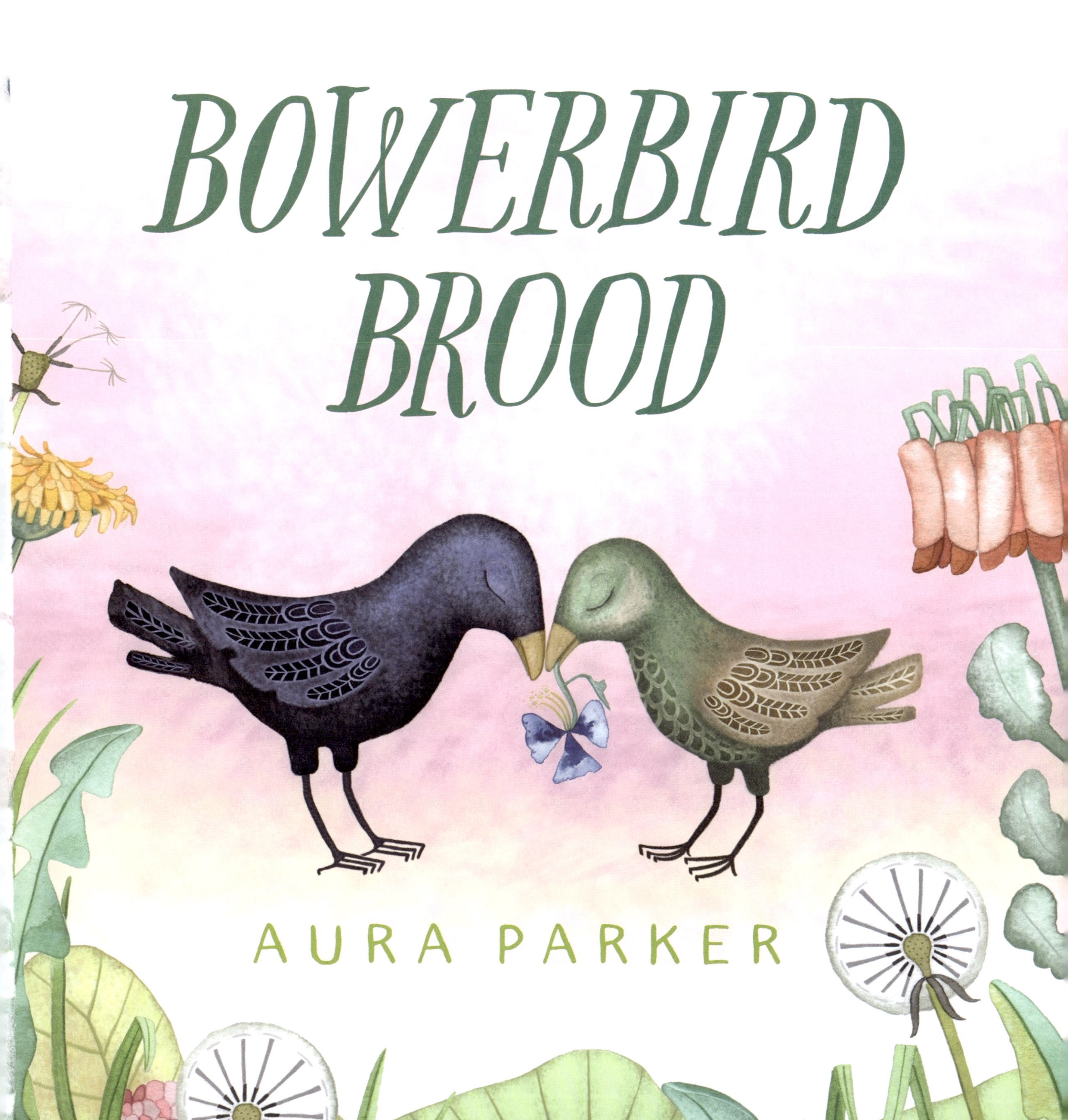

AURA PARKER

For my sister-in-law Michelle Parker
for all the love and care that goes
into her work as a wildlife carer.

Scholastic Press
An imprint of Scholastic Australia Pty Limited (ABN 11 000 614 577)
PO Box 579 Gosford NSW 2250
www.scholastic.com.au

Part of the Scholastic Group
Sydney • Auckland • New York • Toronto • London • Mexico City
New Delhi • Hong Kong • Buenos Aires • Puerto Rico

Published by Scholastic Australia in 2024.

The illustrations created for this book are a mixture of digital and traditional watercolour, with some elements painted by hand on smooth watercolour paper and others with Photoshop brushes.

Book design by Hannah Janzen. Typeset by Astred Hicks.

A catalogue record for this book is available from the National Library of Australia

ISBN: 978-1-76152-162-1

Typeset in Old Claude.

Printed in China by RR Donnelley.

Scholastic Australia's policy, in association with RR Donnelley, is to use papers that are renewable and made efficiently from wood grown in responsibly managed sources, so as to minimise its environmental footprint.

10 9 8 7 6 5 4 3 25 26 27 28 / 2

I am a protector.

Of something small
and wonderful.

Look!

My nest is full.
These fine eggs,
whole and smooth.
My most precious treasures,
safe in your fragile shells.
My perfect three.
But will they hatch?

Always watching,

guarding

and shielding!

When it's cold
my body is a blanket,
wrapping,
warming.

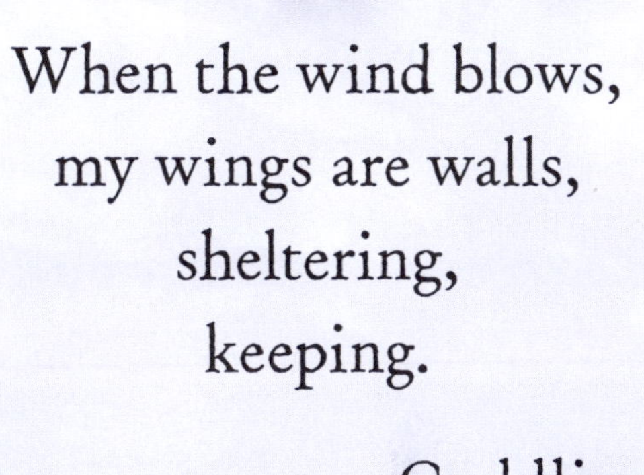

When the wind blows,
my wings are walls,
sheltering,
keeping.

Cuddling,
caring.

Softly,
slowly
stroking,
gently with my feathers.

Whispering,
over and over,

'Little ones,
you are safe
and warm
and loved.'

Through dark days and long shadows.
The sky flashes and cracks open.

Hiding,

blending,

waiting . . .

My eyes grow weary watching the hours pass.
'Safe and warm and loved . . .'

Yearning,

longing.

Brooding,

dreaming.

Wondering.

Have I done enough?

When?

Will you ever hatch?

Tapitty tap.

What's this?

Breaking,

breathing!

Crinkle.

Crick.

CRACK!

Hoping,

HATCHING!

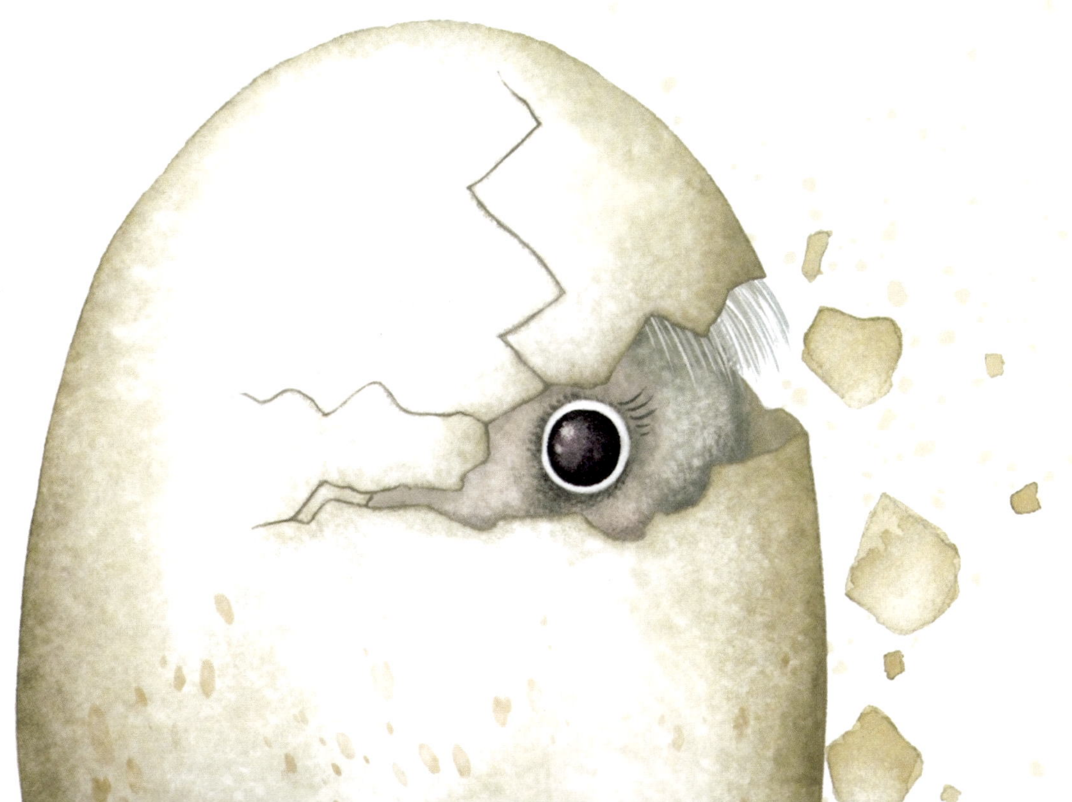

Hello, bright curious eyes,

little spiky head,

soft pink body.

Tiny feet uncurl like a fern.

I stare at the magic of you.

And you!

And you too!

My perfect little hatchlings, three!

Safely in the nest with me.

Cooing,
cradling.

Tending,
waking.

Sleeping,
slurping.

Chuckling,

chirping!

Bumbling,

tumbling.

Happy dancing!

Laughing,

hugging . . .

BELONGING.

Teaching,
sharing
my stories and songs.
Growing,
knowing
they're making you strong.

For now, you are too small to fly.
But I know you want to try . . .

Will you fall in love with the blue of the sky?

Will you adore the deep blue sea?

Where will you go?
What will you see?

Dear little hatchlings, safe with me.
My little fledglings, *stay* with me.

Tottering,

teetering

out of the nest.

'Careful, little ones. The branch is high!'

Stretching,

flexing.

Are you ready?

This is it.

It's time.

Deep breath!

One,

two,

three.

In the sky,
flying
FREE!

Blooming,
bursting
like the bush blossoms.

Squawking,
splashing into the yellow!

Swooping like the swallows

and racing the robins.

Joking with the kookaburras.

Giggling like galahs!

Singing lullabies with the
lyrebirds and lorikeets.

Spying on the powerful owl
on the prowl.

Feasting with the cockatoos.

Breezing by the bowers,
and collecting all the hues.

Through all shades of blue.

I will always love you.

Can you find these?
11 ibis
5 bowerbirds
1 cockatiel
8 brush turkeys
4 rainbow lorikeets